**DreamWorks**

# DRAGONS

## The
## Dragon
## That Rides on
## Lightning

Adapted by Cordelia Evans

Simon Spotlight

New York  London  Toronto  Sydney  New Delhi

SIMON SPOTLIGHT
An imprint of Simon & Schuster Children's Publishing Division
1230 Avenue of the Americas, New York, New York 10020
This Simon Spotlight hardcover edition May 2015
For information about special discounts for bulk purchases,
please contact Simon & Schuster Special Sales at 1-866-506-1949 or business@simonandschuster.com.
Manufactured in China 0215 LEO
2 4 6 8 10 9 7 5 3 1
ISBN 978-1-4814-3613-7
ISBN 978-1-4814-3614-4 (eBook)

Hiccup, Astrid, and Snotlout soared over Berk Sea on their dragons, keeping careful eyes on the water below them.

"We're getting pretty far north," said Astrid, shivering against the cold.

"Bucket and Mulch are two days overdue," Hiccup said. "We need to keep searching."

Just then he spotted their ship in the water next to a glacier—it was being attacked by a ship from the Berserker tribe!

Toothless, Stormfly, and Hookfang blasted the Berserkers until they were forced to retreat.

"What happened here?" Hiccup asked Bucket and Mulch.

"They attacked us because we saw . . . it," Mulch said, leading them over to a wall of ice.

Hiccup rubbed the ice with his sleeve to get a better look. "That looks like a dragon!" he exclaimed.
"Why would Berkserkers be trying to dig it out?" asked Astrid.
"No idea," said Hiccup. "But I'm going to find out."
They cut a block of ice out of the glacier, and the dragons carried the frozen dragon back to Berk.

Hiccup, Astrid, and Fishlegs examined the frozen dragon in the Dragon Training Academy arena. Then they looked for the dragon in the Book of Dragons.

"I think I know why the Berserkers attacked," said Hiccup. "The dragon in the ice is a Skrill."

"Skrills draw lightning from the clouds and then redirect it. They can hit several targets at once," Fishlegs explained.

The Skrill is also the symbol of the Berserker tribe. Dagur, the leader of the Berserkers, was at that moment plotting how to get the Skrill back from Hiccup.

"We will take the Skrill out of Hiccup's frail little hands and destroy that Night Fury!" Dagur declared.

Meanwhile on Berk, Hiccup and the others raced back to the arena only to find that the block of ice had melted—and the Skrill was free and still alive! Toothless and the other dragons surrounded the Skrill, but the Skrill brushed past them easily and launched itself straight up into the clouds above Berk.

"If the Berserkers find that Skrill and know some way to control it . . . ," Stoick began as he watched the Skrill fly away.

"We'll find it first, Dad," Hiccup promised.

But finding the Skrill wasn't easy—not when it could hide itself in the thick clouds. The Dragon Riders tried to force it out, but the Skrill fought them off with bursts of lightning.

To make matters worse, Dagur and the Berserkers appeared and began firing rocks and arrows at Hiccup and his friends from the water below.

"Astrid, take Snotlout and Fishlegs, and try to keep the Berserker ships occupied," Hiccup said. "The twins and I will go after the Skrill."

Hiccup told Ruffnut and Tuffnut his plan for defeating the Skrill: "Basically, you're going to fly blind through the cloud and have Barf let out as much gas as possible. But don't let Belch ignite it until you get to the other side. Hopefully the blast will drive the Skrill out of the clouds, and Toothless can knock it down with a plasma blast."

"That's a lot of gas," said Tuffnut. "Do you have any idea how big a blast that will be?"

"No," said Hiccup.

"Me neither!" said Tuffnut. "How awesome is this?!"

The Skrill was forced out of the clouds by Barf and Belch's blast, but it channeled lightning at Toothless' plasma blast. And then it took off after Ruffnut and Tuffnut!

Hiccup saw the Skrill aiming to attack and arrived just in time for Toothless to fire another plasma blast, this time at very close range.

*BOOM!* The plasma blast hit the Skrill's lightning, creating a massive explosion! The Skrill, Hiccup, and the twins were hurled out of control in different directions.

Ruffnut and Tuffnut landed far away from the others. While they recovered, they watched the Skrill being loaded onto an enemy ship.

"Wait a minute," said Tuffnut. "That's not the Berserkers . . . that's Alvin the Treacherous!"

"Why would Alvin want a Skrill?" asked Ruffnut.

"Why wouldn't he? He could take out Berk with it," said Tuffnut.

"Oh yeah. So we should do something, right?" Ruffnut asked.

"Uh, yes. Yes, we should," said Tuffnut. "I say we follow him."

The other Dragon Riders regrouped on Berk, but no one had seen where the twins went. Hiccup and Toothless set off again in the storm to find them.

"Maybe the twins went after the Skrill," Hiccup said to Toothless. "If we find the Skrill, we find Ruffnut and Tuffnut."

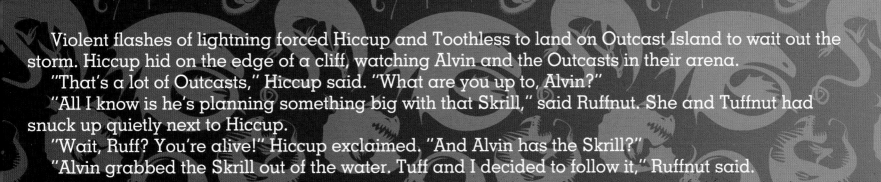

Violent flashes of lightning forced Hiccup and Toothless to land on Outcast Island to wait out the storm. Hiccup hid on the edge of a cliff, watching Alvin and the Outcasts in their arena.

"That's a lot of Outcasts," Hiccup said. "What are you up to, Alvin?"

"All I know is he's planning something big with that Skrill," said Ruffnut. She and Tuffnut had snuck up quietly next to Hiccup.

"Wait, Ruff? You're alive!" Hiccup exclaimed. "And Alvin has the Skrill?"

"Alvin grabbed the Skrill out of the water. Tuff and I decided to follow it," Ruffnut said.

Hiccup and the twins watched as Alvin and the Outcasts harnessed the Skrill. Then Dagur and the Berserkers entered the arena.

"Dagur and Alvin together with the Skrill!" exclaimed Hiccup. "This is really not good. We have to sneak into town and find out what they're up to."

Because Dagur and Alvin would recognize Hiccup, and Ruffnut claimed that Outcast food gave her gas, Tuffnut volunteered to infiltrate the enemy tribes.

Tuffnut got past the guards and into Alvin's throne room, where he listened to Alvin and Dagur form their plan.

"My fleet, led by the glorious Skrill, will lay siege to the Dragon Training arena, and incapacitate Hiccup and his Night Fury," Dagur told Alvin, "while your little fleet of rejects blockades their harbor."

"I don't think so, Dagur," said Alvin. "First, I get Berk. Then, and only then, do you get the Skrill."

Tuffnut hurried back to share what he'd learned.

"The plan is to smash those dirty Berkians to pieces with both fleets! It's going to be awesome!" he said.

"Uh, you do realize we're the Berkians, right?" asked Hiccup.

"Oh right," said Tuffnut. "Still going to be awesome."

"Two fleets and a Skrill are going to be pretty tough to beat," said Hiccup.

"Alvin has made it pretty clear that Dagur doesn't get the Skrill until after they destroy Berk," Tuffnut revealed.

"So no Skrill, no alliance!" said Hiccup. "No alliance, no invasion. We're going to free that Skrill."

Hiccup and Toothless snuck down into the Outcast arena while Tuffnut distracted the guards. But when they got to its pen, the Skrill was already gone!

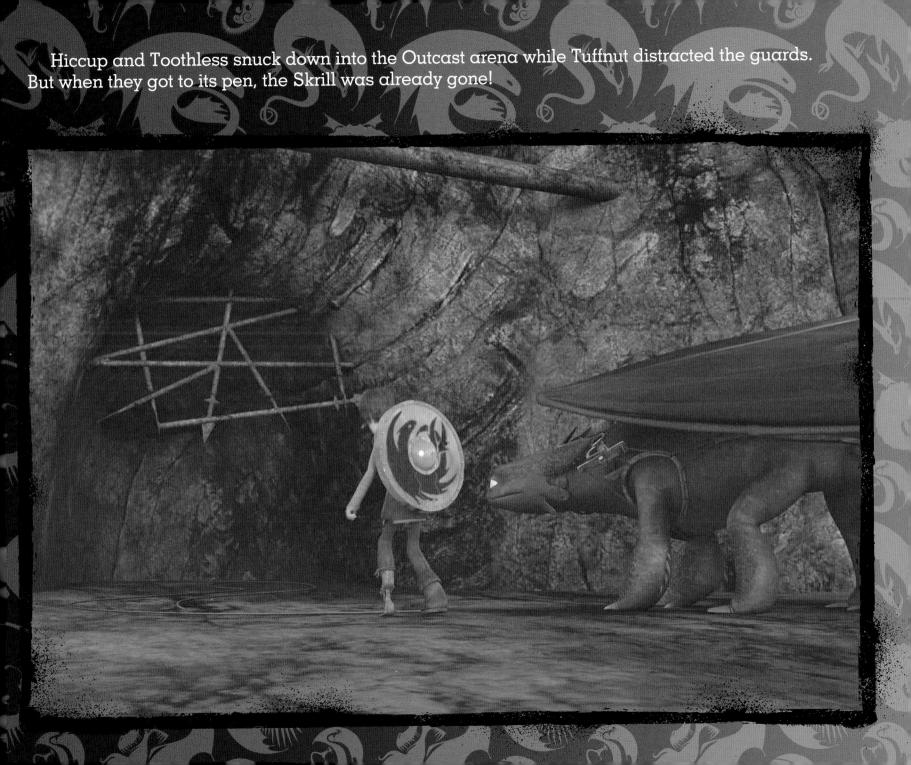

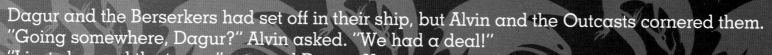

Dagur and the Berserkers had set off in their ship, but Alvin and the Outcasts cornered them. "Going somewhere, Dagur?" Alvin asked. "We had a deal!"

"I just changed the terms," returned Dagur. He cut a rope to let down one of his sails, revealing the Skrill, chained in a harness to the ship!

Alvin tried to fight Dagur, but Dagur made the Skrill shoot lightning blasts at Alvin until he was forced overboard.

Dagur turned to Alvin's fleet of Outcasts. "I have a one-time offer for you and your men: You can join me, or you can join Alvin. Your choice."

A little while later Dagur admired his new fleet of Berserker and Outcast ships. "Now we can lure Hiccup and his Night Fury into battle!" Dagur cried.

"Why wait?" Hiccup called out from above, where he was riding on Toothless. "I thought we could settle this like real Vikings. Just you and me."

"Me and my Skrill against you and your Night Fury," said Dagur, contemplating. "I like those odds."

Hiccup led Dagur to the cliffs, which were full of puddles. They faced off, Hiccup riding Toothless and Dagur harnessing the Skrill above him. Toothless fired a couple of plasma blasts, but the Skrill deflected them with a lightning shield. As Toothless dodged the Skrill's returning blasts, Hiccup watched carefully to make sure Dagur was standing in one of the puddles.

"Any last words, Hiccup?" Dagur threatened.

"I got nothing," Hiccup said. "How about you, bud?" he asked Toothless.

With that, Toothless sent a plasma blast at the Skrill. The Skrill put up its lightning shield to block the blast, which traveled down the ropes, and electrified the water Dagur was standing in.

*ZZZAP!* The blast sent Dagur flying, knocking him out temporarily, and freed the roaring Skrill.

Hiccup may have defeated Dagur, but the Skrill was still chasing him! He and Toothless led the Skrill into a cavernous glacier. Then they hid to one side of a cavern, tricking the Skrill into slamming into their reflection in the ice.

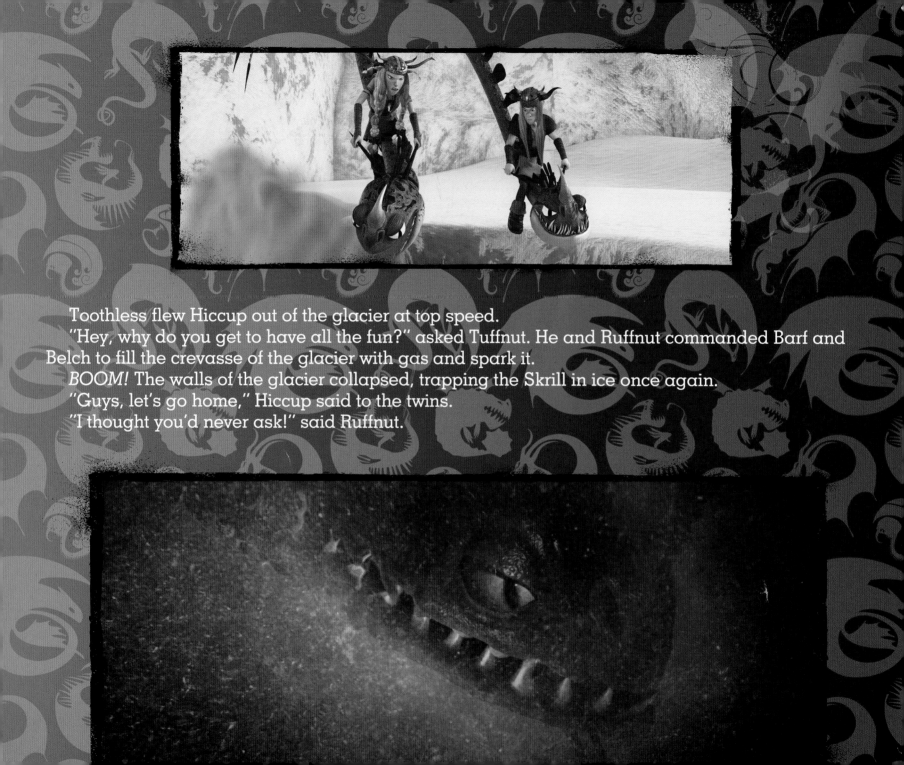

Toothless flew Hiccup out of the glacier at top speed.

"Hey, why do you get to have all the fun?" asked Tuffnut. He and Ruffnut commanded Barf and Belch to fill the crevasse of the glacier with gas and spark it.

*BOOM!* The walls of the glacier collapsed, trapping the Skrill in ice once again.

"Guys, let's go home," Hiccup said to the twins.

"I thought you'd never ask!" said Ruffnut.